BEHIND THE SCENES BIOGRAPHIES

WHAT YOU NEVER KNEW ABOUT

>>>———————————<<<

BLACKPINK

by Mari Bolte

CAPSTONE PRESS
a capstone imprint

This is an unauthorized biography.

Published by Spark, an imprint of Capstone
1710 Roe Crest Drive, North Mankato, Minnesota 56003
capstonepub.com

Copyright © 2025 by Capstone. All rights reserved. No part of this publication
may be reproduced in whole or in part, or stored in a retrieval system, or transmitted in any
form or by any means, electronic, mechanical, photocopying, recording, or otherwise, without
written permission of the publisher.

Library of Congress Cataloging-in-Publication Data
Names: Bolte, Mari, author.
Title: What you never knew about Blackpink / Mari Bolte.
Description: North Mankato, Minnesota : Capstone Press, 2024.
Series: Behind the scenes biographies | Audience: Ages 8 to 11 | Audience: Grades 4-6
Summary: "Their concerts sell out in seconds. They are social media superstars. But that's old news. What don't you know about the K-pop group Blackpink? With high-interest, carefully leveled text, this book goes behind the scenes to bring little-known facts to fans of the hit girl group"-- Provided by publisher.
Identifiers: LCCN 2024006234 (print) | LCCN 2024006235 (ebook) | ISBN 9781669072881 (hardcover) | ISBN 9781669072966 (paperback) | ISBN 9781669072928 (pdf) | ISBN 9781669072973 (epub) | ISBN 9781669072980 (kindle edition)
Subjects: LCSH: Blackpink (Musical group)--Juvenile literature. | Girl groups (Musical groups)--Korea (South)--Juvenile literature.
Classification: LCC ML3930.B579 B65 2024 (print) | LCC ML3930.B579 (ebook) | DDC 782.4216/3095195--dc23/eng/20240209
LC record available at https://lccn.loc.gov/2024006234
LC ebook record available at https://lccn.loc.gov/2024006235

Summary: Learn fun facts about superstar girl group Blackpink, including
how they got their name, where they are from, and more!

Editorial Credits
Editor: Christianne Jones; Designer: Elijah Blue; Media Researcher: Jo Miller; Production Specialist: Whitney Schaefer

Image Credits
Alamy: SOPA Images Limited/Alamy Live News, 23, YG Entertainment/Entertainment Pictures, 10; Getty Images: Chung Sung-Jun, 25, Dimitrios Kambouris, 21, Emma McIntyre, 4, 7, Frazer Harrison, 15, 9, Kevin Winter, 19 (top right), Pool, 17, Rich Fury, 12; Newscom: KCS Presse/MEGA, 13, Lee Young Ho/Sipa USA, 29, UnBoxPHD/SplashNews, 20, Yonhap News/YNA, 11, 26; Shutterstock: Andrea Raffin, 19 (top left), DOCTOR BLACK, 23, (back), Lifestyle Graphic, 23 (bottom), mhatzapa, 18, Naddya, 13 (rose), rafapress, 27, Roger Kisby, cover, Sedanurr, 24, Seymont Studio, 8, stock_photo_world, 19 (bottom), wittaya photo, 22, Zety Akhzar, 14

Design Elements: Shutterstock: IIIerlok_xolms

Any additional websites and resources referenced in this book are not maintained, authorized, or sponsored by Capstone. All product and company names are trademarks™ or registered® trademarks of their respective holders.

TABLE OF CONTENTS

K-Pop Queens 4

Social Media Superstars 8

Girl Power and Respect 12

Cool Collabs 18

Fashion Forward 20

Pretty Savage 24

Making A Change 26

      Glossary 30

      Read More 31

      Internet Sites 31

      Index 32

      About the Author 32

Words in **bold** are in the glossary.

K-POP QUEENS

From left: Lisa, Jisoo, Rosé, Jennie

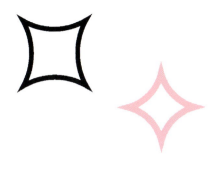

Together, Jennie, Jisoo, Lisa, and Rosé are Blackpink. They are a famous **K-pop** group. Their concerts sell out in seconds. Millions of people watch their music videos.

But that's old news. What don't you know about Blackpink?

How well do you know these K-pop queens? Take the quiz and find out.

1. Which letters of the Blackpink logo are backward?

2. Each member of Blackpink grew up in a different country. Can you name the countries?

3. What entertainment company formed Blackpink?

1. C and N **2.** New Zealand (Jennie); South Korea (Jisoo); Australia (Rosé); Thailand (Lisa) **3.** YG Entertainment

SOCIAL MEDIA SUPERSTARS

The members of Blackpink are social media superstars. They have millions of followers. On YouTube, they have the most-viewed group music channel.

Lisa was the first K-pop star to hit 90 million followers on Instagram. The other members were not far behind!

FACT
Blackpink fans call themselves BLINKs. It's a combo of "black" and "pink."

Their voices and lyrics are one reason fans love them. Their dance moves are another! "Ddu-du Ddu-du" was the first K-pop song to hit one billion views on YouTube.

"Kill This Love" was the most-viewed music video in its first 24 hours. It was watched nearly 57 million times!

GIRL POWER
AND RESPECT

Blackpink is one of the best-selling K-pop girl groups ever. Their 2016 hit "Boombayah" reached number one on *Billboard*'s world digital song sales chart.

In 2023, Jisoo released her first solo album. More than 15.2 million people listened on Spotify. Jisoo became the K-pop soloist with the most monthly listeners. She edged out BTS star Jimin.

Blackpink has led the way in growing the Korean music industry. In 2018, they were the first all-female K-pop group listed on *Billboard's* Emerging Artists chart. In 2022, they made the cover of *Rolling Stone* magazine.

South Korea is a small country. The world of music is even smaller. The members of Blackpink have friends in other K-pop groups. Red Velvet and Blackpink are each other's fans. They have even copied each other's dance moves.

COOL COLLABS

Blackpink has worked with many well-known artists. One is Lady Gaga. She is a role model for the group. They like how she has her own style. It was a huge honor when Lady Gaga personally called them!

FACT
Blackpink has also worked with Cardi B, Ariana Grande, and Dua Lipa. Their **collaborations** have been instant hits.

FASHION
FORWARD

Blackpink members always wear coordinating outfits. But each member brings her own details and tastes. They combine group unity with individual style.

FACT
In 2018, Blackpink won the K-Style Icon award from *Elle* magazine.

The group has played a huge role in bringing traditional Korean **hanbok** to modern fashion. They partnered with hanbok designer Kim Danha in 2020. The brand had a 3,000-percent increase in sales!

Models showcase hanbok in Seoul, South Korea

Kim Danha

PRETTY SAVAGE

Blackpink is a memorable group name. The group came up with it together. They picked two colors that represent them best. Pink is considered pretty, girly, and light. Black is considered powerful, savage, and dark.

MAKING A CHANGE

Blackpink uses their fame to help change the world. The United Nations (UN) called on them to ask young people to protect the planet. The members are the first Asian artists in this role for the UN.

FACT
Blackpink made a video called "Climate Action in Your Area!" It encouraged fans to take action against climate change.

27

The environment isn't the only issue the group cares about. The members have donated money to **disaster relief** after heavy floods and fires.

In 2020, the **COVID-19 pandemic** took over the world. Blackpink designed special face masks to sell. The money went to charity. Another 50,000 masks were sent across the United States.

Glossary

collaboration (kuh-lah-buh-RAY-shuhn)—project produced by two or more people

COVID-19 (KO-vid nine-TEEN)—a mild to severe respiratory illness that is caused by a coronavirus

disaster relief (dih-ZAH-stuhr rih-LEEF)—help provided after an event that caused great damage, destruction, or loss

hanbok (HAHN-boh)—traditional Korean clothing

K-pop (KAY-pahp)—a style of popular music that began in South Korea

pandemic (pan-DEH-mik)—a disease that spreads over a wide area and affects many people

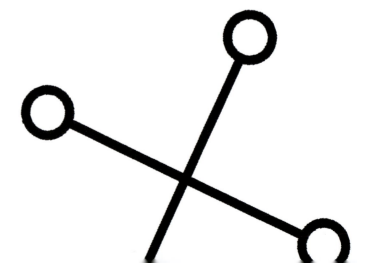

Read More

Andrews, Elizabeth. *Jung Kook: BTS Singer and Beyond*. Minneapolis: ABDO, 2023.

Brown, Helen. *Blackpink: Queens of K-Pop*. New York: Sterling Children's Books, 2020.

Stevens, Cara J. *Blackpink: Pretty Isn't Everything*. New York: HarperCollins, 2019.

Internet Sites

Blackpink Official Site
ygfamily.com/en/artists/blackpink/main

Kiddle: Blackpink Facts for Kids
kids.kiddle.co/Blackpink

KidzSearch: Blackpink
wiki.kidzsearch.com/wiki/Blackpink

Index

Billboard's Emerging Artists, 14
BLINKs, 9

charity, 28
climate change, 27
collaborations, 18

hanbok, 22
home countries, 6

K-Style Icon award, 21

logo, 6

music videos, 5
  "Climate Action in Your Area!", 27
  "Kill This Love", 11

Red Velvet, 16, 17
Rolling Stone magazine, 14

social media
  Instagram, 8
  YouTube, 8

songs
  "Boombayah", 12
  "Ddu-du Ddu-du", 10
Spotify, 13
style, 21

United Nations (UN), 27

About the Author

Mari Bolte is a Korean adoptee and the mom of a huge K-pop fan. She is also the author and editor of hundreds of children's books. Every book is her favorite book as long as the readers learned something and enjoyed themselves!